P9-CEE-598

Sometimes I'm
BOMBALOO

by **Rachel Vail**

illustrated by **Yumi Heo**

SCHOLASTIC INC.

New York Toronto London Auckland Sydney
Mexico City New Delhi Hong Kong Buenos Aires

No part of this publication may be reproduced, stored
in a retrieval system, or transmitted in any form or by any
means, electronic, mechanical, photocopying, recording,
or otherwise, without written permission of the publisher.
For information regarding permission, write to Scholastic
Inc., Attention: Permissions Department, 557 Broadway,
New York, NY 10012.

ISBN 0-439-66941-3

Text copyright © 2002 by Rachel Vail.
Illustrations copyright © 2002 by Yumi Heo.

All rights reserved. Published by Scholastic Inc.
SCHOLASTIC and associated logos are trademarks
and/or registered trademarks of Scholastic Inc.

30 29   18 19/0

Printed in the U.S.A.   40

First Bookshelf edition, February 2005

Book design by Kristina Albertson

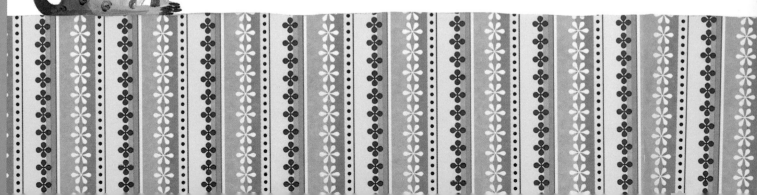

To my friend, Lauren.

R.V.

To my son, Auden.

Y.H.

My name is Katie Honors and I'm a really good kid.
I smile a lot because usually I'm happy,
and I give excellent hugs.

I brush my teeth

without being reminded, too much.

I
can
Velcro
my own
shoes,

and put my toys where they belong, including the ones

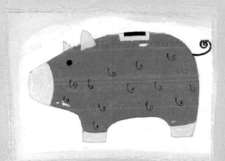  

with sixty-forty-eight small pieces.

I remember about using my napkin,

and the magic word.

I don't whine or stamp my feet or growl,
even if my brother knocks down my beautiful castle
I just built and I told him not to touch it and I'll
never be able to get it to look that good again.

Sometimes I can hold in the tears and the pushes, and just say, "That's okay."

But sometimes I'm Bombaloo.

I show my teeth and make fierce noises.

My face scrunches tight like a monster's.

I use my feet and

my fists instead of my words.

My toys end up all over the floor—

and

so does my brother.

There is a lot of yelling
when I'm Bombaloo,

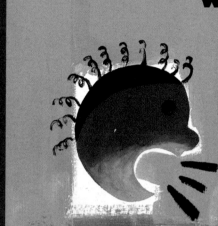

and some pointing at my bed.

I have

to go take

some time for myself

and think about it.

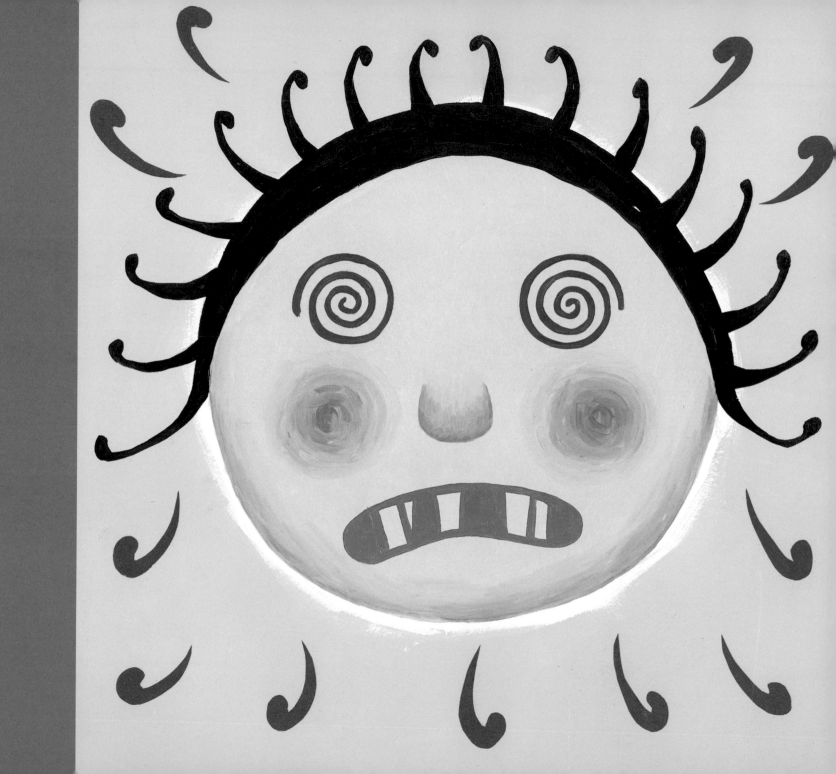

But when I'm Bombaloo, I don't want to think about it. I want to smash stuff.

I can come out when I'm ready to control
myself and say I'm sorry to my brother. But
while I'm **Bombaloo**, I'm not sorry;
I'm angry. I hate everybody and everything,
even my dog, Vanilla, and my penny collection
and my blankie and my mother and all of
the clothes in my drawers.

On their way out of the drawer

a pair of underpants lands on my head.
Like a hat.
When I laugh I'm Katie Honors again.

And I'm sorry and a little frightened.

It's scary, being Bombaloo.

My mother knows that.

She hugs me

and helps me clean up the mess Bombaloo made,

and then after some sorries and kisses for my brother,

we build a new castle

together.